This book belongs to

....

Walt Disney's
The Sorcerer's Apprentice

Storybook Favourites

Reader's Digest Young Families

Walt Disney's The Sorcerer's Apprentice

Illustrations by The Walt Disney Studios

Once there was a man who knew everything there was to know about magic.

He was a great sorcerer.

He brewed potions that could make camels talk.

He transformed pebbles into rubies and diamonds.

He made the stars shoot across the sky and burst onto the ground wherever he directed them.

And the sorcerer had a wonderful hat.

When he wore his hat, all he had to do was just think magic and it would happen.

He could think about a butterfly and it would appear.

But only the sorcerer knew the magic words that would make it disappear.

The sorcerer did not live alone.

Surely he could not tend to his castle and still have time for his brilliant sorcery.

He had a helper.

His helper's name was Mickey.

And Mickey did all the work.

Mickey did not help with the sorcery.
But he swept the floor.
He chopped the wood.
He carried the water from the fountain to the vat.

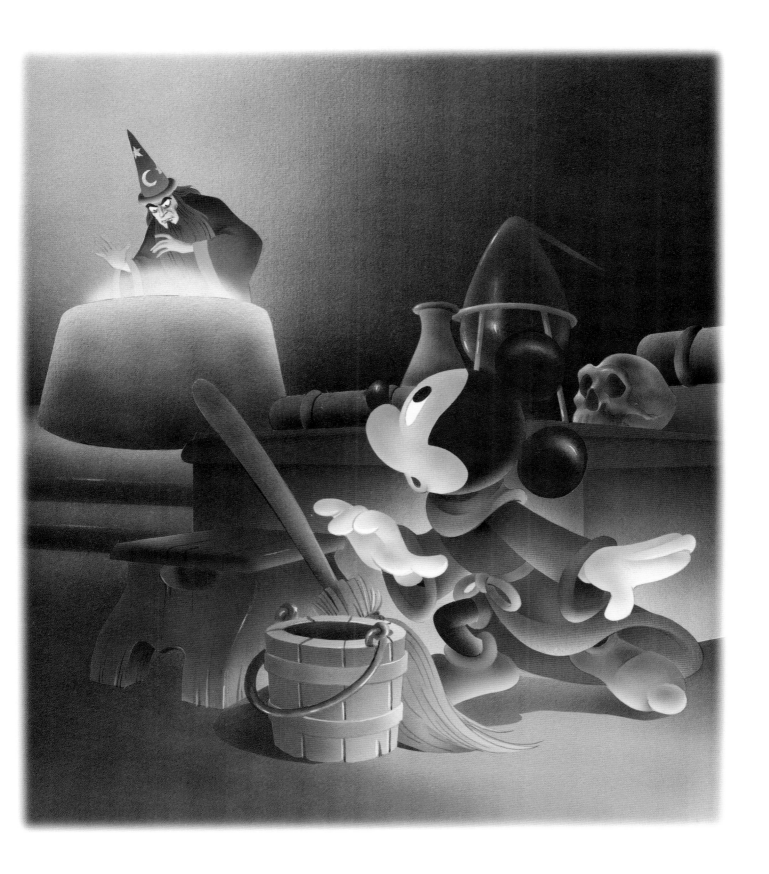

Mickey knew about the magic of the hat.

'If I had that hat,' thought Mickey, 'I would never have to work again.'

One day the sorcerer had to go out.
Mickey was left all alone.
And there on the table was the sorcerer's magic hat.
The sorcerer had left it behind.
The temptation was too great for Mickey.

Mickey looked longingly at the magic hat.
Ever so slowly, he reached for it.
Ever so gently, he took it off the table.
Ever so carefully, he raised it into the air.
Ever so proudly, he lowered it onto his head.
'Now I can be a sorcerer,' Mickey said to himself. 'The magic hat is all I need.'

An old broom was leaning against the wall.

'I will put a spell on that broom,' said Mickey. 'That's a good place to start.'

And Mickey did what the sorcerer always did. He pointed his fingers straight at the broom. And the broom began to move.

Suddenly the broom had two feet . . . then a right arm . . . and then a left arm.

'Broom!' commanded Mickey. 'Pick up the buckets!'

The broom did just what Mickey said.

'Broom!' ordered Mickey. 'Go up the steps.' The broom went up the steps.

'Fill the buckets,' ordered Mickey. The broom filled the buckets.

'Bring them back down,' ordered Mickey. The broom brought them back.

'Pour the water into the vat,' ordered Mickey. The broom poured the water into the vat.

Mickey danced around the room.
'Magic is easy!' he cried. 'I will never have to work again!'
Then Mickey sat down in the sorcerer's chair.
'Work, broom, work!' he ordered. While the broom went up and down the steps, filling buckets and pouring water, Mickey fell sound asleep.
He dreamed he was the greatest sorcerer in the world.

Suddenly something cold and wet woke Mickey up. It was a splash of water.

Another splash knocked Mickey out of the chair.

Mickey looked around. Water was everywhere!

The vat was overflowing and the broom was flooding the
room.
'Stop!' cried Mickey. 'Stop, broom! Stop, I say!'
But the broom did not stop.

Mickey pointed his finger at the broom. But the broom kept going.

Mickey held out his arms.

But the broom pushed him down.

Mickey grabbed the buckets.

But the broom held on tight.

Wasn't there any way to stop the broom?

The axe! Mickey grabbed it.
He chopped the broom into bits.
'Well, that's over!' said Mickey.

But it wasn't over.
Something strange was going on.
The bits of wood began to move.
The bits of wood turned into brooms.
All the new brooms had feet and arms and buckets.
And they all marched up the steps, never stopping.

The brooms came down the steps with more water.
Mickey held out his arms to hold them back.
But the brooms walked right over him.
'I am a sorcerer!' cried Mickey. 'You must do as I say!'
But the brooms marched on and on.

Brooms and brooms and more brooms!
Buckets and buckets and more buckets!
In a great line, they poured more and more water into the vat.
And the vat kept overflowing.
The water got deeper and deeper.
Poor Mickey!
It was all he could do to keep himself above the water.

Then the sorcerer's *Book of Magic* floated by, and Mickey grabbed it.

He turned page after page after page, looking for the magic words that would stop the brooms.

But the water began to whirl. Mickey could no longer read the words.

Mickey hung onto the book as he went around and around in the water. Spinning faster and faster, he was caught in a great whirlpool.

Now there was nothing he could do.

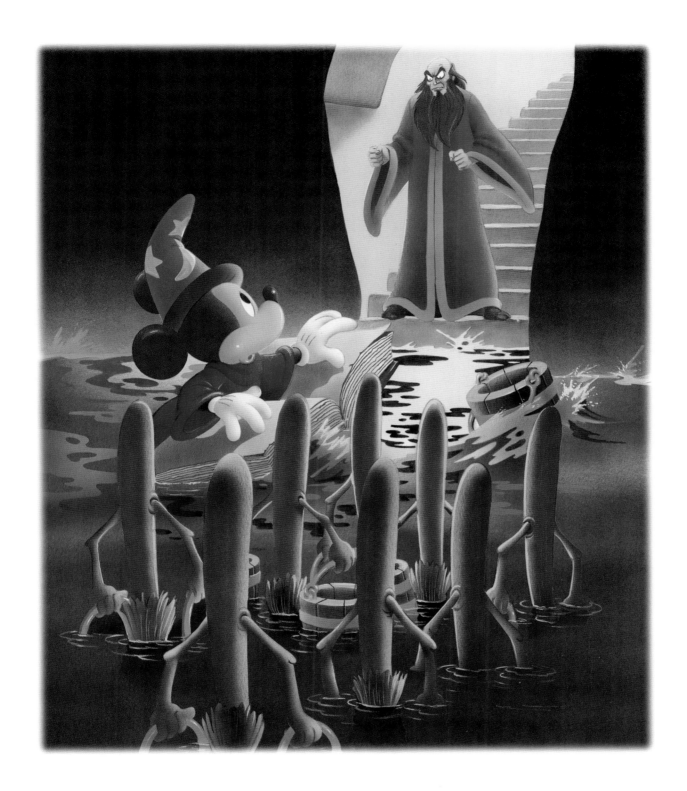

A bright light suddenly filled the room.

What was this?

The sorcerer had returned, and he knew at once what Mickey had done.

He raised his arms and roared a great command.

Instantly the water and the brooms disappeared – except for one broom. It was the old broom, still leaning against the wall.

The sorcerer was frowning as he looked down at Mickey.

Mickey took off the sorcerer's hat. Very carefully and ever so neatly, he tried to make the magic hat look nice again. Then he gave it back to the sorcerer.

'Just a little magic trick, ha, ha!' said Mickey.

But the sorcerer did not laugh. Again, he looked down at his little helper. 'Don't ever start what you can't finish,' he said.

So Mickey went up the steps and back to work.

Walt Disney's The Sorcerer's Apprentice is a *Disney Storybook Favourites* book

Walt Disney's The Sorcerer's Apprentice, copyright © 1973, 2006 Disney Enterprises, Inc.
Illustrated by The Walt Disney Studios

This edition was adapted and published in 2009 by
The Reader's Digest Association Limited
11 Westferry Circus, Canary Wharf, London E14 4HE

Editor: Rachel Warren Chadd
Designer: Louise Turpin
Design consultant: Simon Webb

® Reader's Digest, the Pegasus logo and Reader's Digest Young Families
are registered trademarks of
The Reader's Digest Association, Inc.

We are committed both to the quality of our products
and the service we provide to our customers.
We value your comments, so please do contact us on
08705 113366 or via our website at
www.readersdigest.co.uk
If you have any comments or suggestions
about the content of our books, email us at
gbeditorial@readersdigest.co.uk

Printed in China

A Disney Enterprises/Reader's Digest Young Families Book

ISBN 978 0 276 44472 2
Book code 641-031 UP0000-1
Oracle code 504400087H.00.24